BRIEF THIEF

Written by Michaël Escoffier • Illustrated by Kris Di Giacomo

For Evan - M.E.

ENCHANTED LION BOOKS

NEW YORK

This morning Leon enjoyed his breakfast.

Then he sunned himself
on a big rock.

And now, Leon has to go poo.

He finds a nice tree
to hide behind.

But when he's done,
he realizes ... OH NO!
NO PAPER!

Leon looks around
for something to use.

Leaves?
No, they're too prickly.

Grass?
No, that will be too messy.

But wait! These old underpants
here will do the trick!

They might belong to someone...
But who would come all the way up here?

And anyway, they're full of holes.

Leon finishes his business.

Then he throws
the underpants into the bushes
and goes back to his rock.

HEY! who do you think you are?

Huh? What? Who said that?

Yeah, you there. You think I didn't see that?

It's me, your conscience.

My conscience?
What's that?

I'm the little voice
you hear inside your head
whenever you get up
to something naughty.

But I didn't do anything!

Are you sure? One hundred percent sure?
Cross-your-heart sure?

Well... There were those underpants...

Aha! Now we're getting somewhere!
Since when are we allowed to touch
other people's things?
What DO they teach you in school, anyway?

It was just an old pair
of underpants full of holes.
I thought they'd been
thrown away...

Oh, you THOUGHT that, did you?!
But did you also think that maybe
the OWNEr of those underpants
could have lost them?
Or that maybe SOMEONE stole them from him?
Or that maybe, just maybe, he had washed them
and gone off for a walk in the woods
while they were hanging out in the sun to dry?

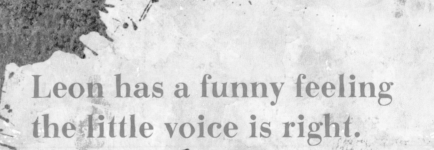

Leon has a funny feeling
the little voice is right.

You know what you need to do now?
Go on, scrub! Like you mean it!
I don't want to see a single trace left.

AND WHEN YOU'VE FINISHED, hang them up to dry and

GET LOST !!

Old underpants
full of holes,
indeed!

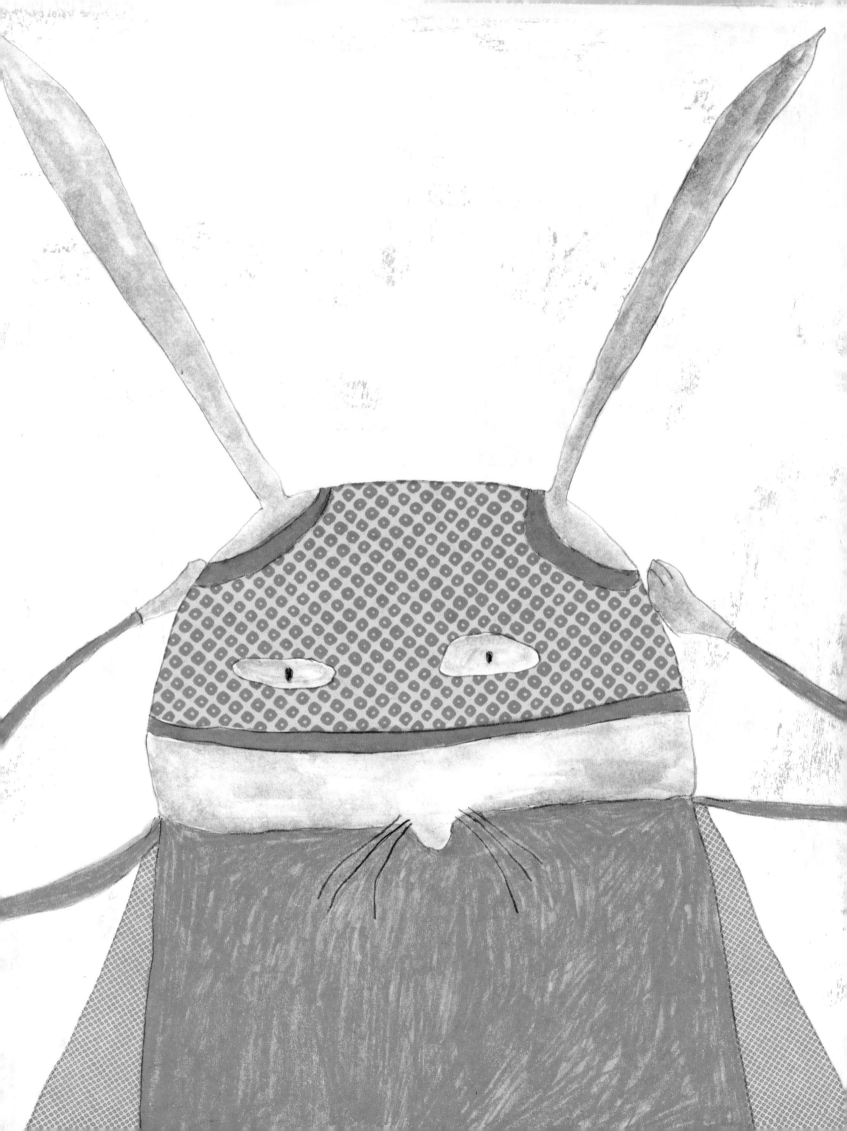